Enid Blyton's
NODDY
Loses Sixpence

BBC BOOKS

It was a beautiful morning in Toyland. Noddy was looking forward to a busy day driving passengers to and fro in his little car.

"Good morning, Mr Milko, it's a lovely day," said Noddy.

Mr Milko looked miserable. "It's a sad day for me, Noddy," he said. "I've lost my special watch."

"Well, I shall look for your watch wherever I go," said Noddy.

"Thank you, Noddy," said the milkman. "There's a reward of sixpence for whoever finds it." He rang Noddy's bell, but even that didn't cheer him up, and he trudged off.

Noddy drove to the market square to collect the Pink Cat.

"Take me to the station, driver," she commanded. Noddy told the Pink Cat that her fare would be sixpence, and she settled herself in the car, squashing Noddy.

"You'll have to put your tail inside the car," said Noddy.

The Pink Cat frowned, but she tucked her tail in. "Do start," she fussed, "or I shall miss my train."

Noddy drove so fast over the bumps that the Pink Cat's tail flopped out of the car again.

"Oh, do please put your tail back, Pink Cat,"
said Noddy.

But the Pink Cat ignored him. Noddy was
cross.

"I wish cats would look after their tails,"
he grumbled.

Suddenly, the Pink Cat's tail got caught in the wheel, and it fell off on to the road.

Noddy and the Pink Cat didn't notice, but someone else did.

"Just in time," said Noddy, as they arrived at the station. "Can I have my fare, please?"

But as she got out of the car, the Pink Cat spun around. "Oh, no," she cried. "My tail's gone. *I'm* not paying you. You owe *me* sixpence for a new tail." And off she flounced.

Noddy sat miserably in his car. But then Dinah Doll arrived. She wanted to be taken to Toy Town to open her market stall. Noddy cheered up at once. "We'll balance your bag on the back of the car," he said. "I haven't got a strap to tie it down."

Dinah Doll thought Noddy's car was
beautiful. "But please go faster," she urged.
"Parp! Parp!" said the car, as it
went at top speed. As it drove over
a bump, Dinah Doll's bag
toppled into the road and was
left behind.

Noddy's car screeched to a halt near Dinah Doll's stall. But as he got out, Noddy noticed that Dinah Doll's bag was missing. "Oh dear," he said.

"You're very careless, Noddy," said Dinah Doll. "My special blue purse was in there."

Noddy offered to look for the bag. Dinah
Doll was very cross. "I can't pay you now,"
she said. "In fact, if you don't find my bag
you'll have to pay *me* sixpence."

Poor Noddy. He sat on the pavement beside
his car. "Parp! Parp!" it said sadly.

Noddy searched the roadside for the Pink Cat's tail and Dinah Doll's bag. "Oh dear," he said. "I need a friend to help me."

And just at that moment, Big-Ears turned up on his bicycle.

"What are you doing, little Noddy?" he asked.

"Oh, Big-Ears," cried Noddy. "You're my friend."

Big-Ears was puzzled. "I know that," he said.

So Noddy told Big-Ears how he'd had two passengers. "But I lost Pink Cat's fluffy tail and Dinah Doll's bag, so they won't pay me. And now I've got to pay *them* sixpences. What shall I do, Big-Ears?"

Big-Ears thought...

"When you've lost something and you can't find it," he said, "someone else has usually found it. We must go back to Toy Town and look for someone with a fluffy tail and a new bag."

"Oh, yes," said Noddy. "Let's go now, Big-Ears."

So off they went.

Back in Toy Town, Martha Monkey strolled up to Dinah Doll's stall. She was looking very smart with a new pink scarf around her neck.

"Where did you get it?" asked Dinah Doll.

"Oh, it just came my way," said Martha Monkey.

Martha didn't notice that Noddy and Big-Ears were watching her. She sat grandly down at a café table, where everyone could admire her new scarf.

"That's the Pink Cat's tail," whispered Noddy to Big-Ears. "Fancy wearing it as a scarf!"

"That's not your scarf," Big-Ears told Martha
Monkey sternly.

"Yes it is. I…I found it," she stammered.

"That is the Pink Cat's tail," insisted Big-Ears.
"And she wants it back."

"She can't have it," retorted Martha rudely.
"She shouldn't leave it lying around."

"If you don't give it back," said Big-Ears, "she'll scratch you with her sharp claws. And she'll hiss at you."

Martha Monkey looked nervous. She took the tail off and dropped it on the table. "Yes, that's just the sort of horrid thing she would do," she said sulkily.

Martha Monkey hurried off, and Noddy
picked up the tail.

"Oh, thank you, Big-Ears," he said.

"Now we must find Dinah Doll's bag," said
Big-Ears. "We must look around very carefully."

The Clockwork Mouse was chattering to Mr Sparks. There was something red on the table between them.

Noddy and Big-Ears moved closer.

"I'm going on holiday," the Clockwork Mouse was saying, "with my beautiful new bag. The only thing is, I don't know how to open it."

At that moment Big-Ears popped up from behind a table.

"Please, allow me," he offered.

Big-Ears took the bag and opened it.

"I thought so," he said. "Here's Dinah Doll's special blue purse."

Then Noddy appeared.
"Oh, yes," he said. "That's
Dinah Doll's bag all right."
With a squeak of fear the
Clockwork Mouse was gone.

"Look," said Big-Ears, and he picked
something up from the Clockwork Mouse's
chair. "He's dropped something else. A watch."

"A watch?" repeated Noddy. "Mr Milko lost his
watch. What time does it say?"

"Six o'clock," said Big-Ears, peering at the
watch.

"Why, that's the time Mr Milko starts his round. It must be his watch!" exclaimed Noddy. "I'll give it back to him. And now I can give Dinah Doll her bag and the Pink Cat her tail. Oh, thank you, Big-Ears!"

Next morning, Mr Milko arrived as usual.
He put a bottle of milk on Noddy's
doorstep.

"Good morning," said Noddy.

But Mr Milko was still
miserable. "No, it's not…"
he began.

"But it is," said Noddy. "Yesterday I lost Dinah Doll's bag and the Pink Cat's tail. But Big-Ears and I found them again. They were so pleased, they each gave me two sixpences. So today we're going to have a huge tea-party."

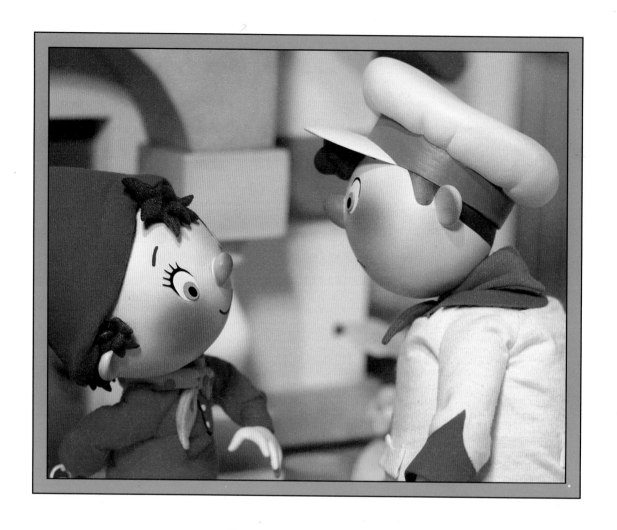

"Oh," said Mr Milko. "Good."
"And we found something else,"
beamed Noddy. He held out
Mr Milko's watch.

28

"Oh, Noddy, you are clever. I shall give you two sixpences as well."

"Oooh!" exclaimed Noddy. "We shall have an ENORMOUS tea-party."

"I'm so happy," smiled Mr Milko. "I'd love to ring your little bell, Noddy."

"All right," said Noddy. "Carry on, Mr Milko."

So Mr Milko tapped Noddy's head.
His little bell rang and rang, as
Mr Milko disappeared, whistling
a happy tune.

Other Noddy *TV Tie-in titles*
available from BBC Children's Books

Noddy and his Bell
Noddy and the Goblins
Noddy and Martha Monkey
Noddy and the Naughty Tail
Noddy and his New Friend
Noddy and the Kite
Noddy and the Pouring Rain

Other TV Tie-in titles in preparation

Noddy and the Broken Bicycle
Noddy Delivers Some Parcels
Noddy Gets a New Job
Noddy and the Milkman
Noddy and the Special Key

Published by BBC Books
a division of BBC Enterprises Limited
Woodlands, 80 Wood Lane, London W12 0TT
First published 1992
Reprinted 1992
Text and stills copyright © BBC Enterprises Limited 1992
ISBN 0 563 36852 7

Based on the Television series, produced by
Cosgrove Hall Productions, inspired by the Noddy Books
which are copyright Darrell Waters Limited 1949-1968

Enid Blyton's signature and Noddy are Trademarks of Darrell Waters Limited

Designed and typeset in 17/21pt Garamond by Between the Lines, London

Printed and bound in Great Britain by Cambus Limited, East Kilbride
Colour separations by DOT Gradations, Chelmsford
Cover printed by Cambus Limited, East Kilbride